The Ink Drinker

story by ÉRIC SANVOISIN
illustrations by MARTIN MATJE

LE BUVEUR D'ENCRE
translated by GEORGES MOROZ

A Dell Yearling Book

35 Years of Exceptional Reading

Dell Yearling Books
Established 1966

Published by
Dell Yearling
an imprint of
Random House Children's Books
a division of Random House, Inc.
1540 Broadway
New York, New York 10036

Text copyright © 1996 by Éric Sanvoisin
Illustrations copyright © 1996 by Martin Matje
Translation copyright © 1998 by Georges Moroz

First American Edition 1998
Originally published by Les Éditions Nathan, Paris, 1996

Visit us on the Web! www.randomhouse.com/kids

Educators and librarians, for a variety of teaching tools, visit us at www.randomhouse.com/teachers

ISBN: 0-440-41485-7

Reprinted by arrangement with Delacorte Press

Printed in the United States of America

February 2002

10 9 8 7 6 5 4

For our little #6.

The Ink
Drinker

one

The Hiding Place

My father owns a bookstore. He loves books. He devours them like an ogre. All day and long into the night, he reads. It's an obsession. There's no cure, but our family doctor doesn't seem to worry.

Every evening, I find a new pile of books at our home. They're everywhere—even in the bathrooms. But it's useless to complain. With

Dad, books are always welcome. He speaks to them as though they were people. He gives them first names and calls them "my little bookies." Every book is his special friend.

As for me, I have no special friend. And books definitely don't qualify. I hate them. You see, I may look like my dad, but deep inside we are very different people. Mom pretends not to notice this because she loves us both. Can you believe that she won't even come to my rescue when Dad forces me to read?

Summer vacation has just started and, to keep busy, I'm helping in the bookstore. I'm not allowed to do much, though. Dad won't let me tidy up or even touch anything. He says paper doesn't last long in my hands. I guess I do like the sound of paper being torn. It's like music to my ears.

So I watch out for shoplifters. It's the only fun thing to do in the bookstore. But each time a book ends up in the pocket of a thief, I keep quiet. It pleases me to know that there's one less book! The problem is, there are hardly any shoplifters, since my dad almost always spots a thief as soon as one enters the store.

I end up spending most of my time observing the customers. I know all the regulars and all their little habits. Some sniff the books as though they were selecting a bouquet of roses. Some choose any old book because they love a surprise. And still others can't make up their minds. They pick up a book, put it back, take it again, and finally leave it. More often than not, those who walk away empty-handed look all embarrassed because they haven't bought anything.

I have a hiding spot in the back of the store, a tiny window carved in a wall of books. No one can see me. I am a spy. I write down the tiniest details of my observations in a notebook. Who knows, it might be the starting point for my very own book! But I doubt it because grammar isn't my strong point.

Today there was a new customer whom I'd never seen before. He must have just moved to the neighborhood. He was one weird-looking guy, with a gray complexion and bristly eyebrows. His behavior was even weirder. I could hardly believe my eyes—it looked as if he was floating off the ground like a ghost!

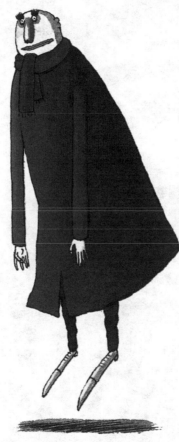

two

A Strange Customer

With my very own eyes I saw the unknown reader drinking a book! I'm not kidding. And I swear I wasn't hallucinating. For five minutes I saw him walking silently between the shelves, with his eyes closed and his arms stretched out in front of him. It was as though he were listening to the sound of the books.

All of a sudden he seized one. Then things got even crazier.

He didn't open the book. He simply separated the middle pages and created a slit. Through this slit he inserted a straw, which he took out of his pocket, and he started sucking on it. A look of absolute pleasure spread over his face, as if the book contained an ice-cream soda. To be sure, it was a super-hot day, definitely not weather for book shopping.

I gasped in surprise. That was a mistake. The strange customer obviously heard me because he quickly reshelved the book, put the

8

straw back in his pocket and headed straight for the door.

As soon as he was gone, I jumped out of my hiding spot and went to examine the book in which he had inserted the straw. It was easy enough to find because the book was thin and had a rubberlike texture. As I pulled it off the shelf, I was struck by its incredible lightness. If there had been a gust of wind, the book would have blown away.

But that wasn't all. When I opened the book, I almost fainted. It was blank. There wasn't a single word left on the pages! The weird reader had drunk the ink of the book down to nearly the very last letter. . . .

three

The Chase

I was so excited that I didn't have time to be afraid. I had to take action—and fast! I was convinced the strange customer would never come back to the store, since he had heard me gasp and knew that someone had caught him drinking ink.

I had two choices: either I could tell my dad everything I'd just seen, or I could figure this thing out on my own like a real detective. I knew my father would never believe me anyway. He might even accuse me of erasing the letters one by one. After all, he knows I'm allergic to reading. So I decided to follow the tracks of this odd reader.

"Where are you off to?" Dad asked as I dashed toward the door.

"Just out!" I called back.

In the street, the glare and heat of the sun hit me full blast, and I was afraid I had taken too much time making up my mind. The ink drinker had vanished.

I started to run, weaving in and out among the pedestrians, and raced up the block. Nothing! But giving up was out of the question. This was clearly a once-in-a-lifetime adventure.

I persisted in my chase and finally caught sight of my customer. Instantly I recognized his peculiar looks and his unmistakable walk: he was moving quickly, but his legs were motionless. Everyone in the street steered clear of him.

I stopped behind a tree to catch my breath and then followed in his tracks.

And that's how I ended up in front of the cemetery. . . .

four

In the Cemetery

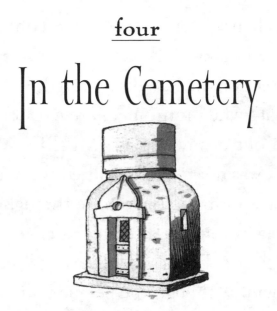

I couldn't help shivering. A cemetery isn't exactly my favorite place to visit, and I knew that if I kept on following him, I might end up in terrible danger.

But I couldn't stop now! I'm a tough kid, not a coward.

I tried to keep up with him as he ran down a path that cut across the middle of the cemetery. Then suddenly he veered off onto a little diagonal walkway. By the time I arrived at the intersection, he had disappeared.

That's when it hit me. A seven-letter word came out of my lips. *VAMPIRE!* What an idiot I was not to have realized this instantly!

Not wanting to have gone through all this trouble in vain, I started to search among the tombstones. Dates and names were engraved on them. Although the people buried underground were unknown to me, I felt uneasy— and impolite as well—to be walking above their resting places.

Yet one of the dead had drunk a book. Where was my vampire hiding? Coming face to face with a vampire is pretty unusual; on top of that, I'd been lucky enough to find a rare *ink*-sucking one. Lucky—and scared to death!

Suddenly I saw it! A strange vaulted monument stood in the middle of the path. It resembled the shape of an ink bottle!

My knees began to tremble. It was still daylight outside, but it might as well have been pitch black.

Moving like a robot, I pushed the gate of the bizarre vaulted grave. It wasn't locked. A flight of stairs went down, deep into the ground. Slowly I descended the steps as cobwebs fell from the ceiling and landed in my hair. Brrr . . .

Downstairs I saw a little round room whose walls were covered with thousands of books, all tightly packed like little soldiers at attention.

17

This strange library was the monster's *pantry*.

A few candles lit a fountain pen—shaped casket that was lying on a platform. And inside . . . well, my customer was snoring.

His body was hidden by a blanket. Only his head, which was resting on a large satin pillow, lay exposed. I noticed that small freckle-like letters seemed to be engraved on his papier-mâché skin. I got closer so that I could examine him in better detail.

Suddenly he sat up and fixed his eyes on me. They were dark with ink.

My blood began to churn. I felt as jumbly as a soft-boiled egg. And I wondered if vampires liked their eggs soft-boiled. . . .

five

Vam . . . Vampire!

I was so frightened I couldn't move. My vocal cords even froze. I was unable to scream.

"What are you doing here, kid?"

The vampire had a soft, hissing voice. I needed a clever reply, and fast. . . .

"I wanted to visit my grandmother's grave. Guess I'm in the wrong place."

"Your grandmother is buried in this cemetery?"

"Well, no. I must have come to the wrong cemetery, too."

He started growling. I was completely startled—especially by the sharp and threatening tongue that moved between his lips. It had the texture of an ink blotter.

"You followed me from the bookstore, kid! Why?"

There was no point in lying anymore. I was sure that he could read my thoughts.

"You drank a book with a straw," I answered. "I saw you!"

"Now I understand. You're a foolish kid. Do you know who I am?"

"A vam—a vampire."

"Indeed. You are lucky that after five centuries of fine dining on blood, I became allergic to the stuff. Otherwise . . ."

I did not dare to think about what he meant.

"Why do you drink ink, sir?" I asked.

"I've suffered from liver problems for seventy-two years. Ink is the only food I can digest without difficulty. And, believe it or not, it is quite nutritious."

"Really? But then why not just buy bottles full of ink? You could keep a refrigerator stocked with them right here in this crypt. It would be a lot easier."

"Not possible, kid. Bottled ink is as bland as salt-free food. But ink that has aged on paper, well, it's the ultimate gourmet dish. Simply sublime."

I frowned.

"You don't believe me?"

"Oh, no. I do. I do!"

I started to back away.

"No, you don't believe me. Never mind, like it or not, you too will develop a taste for ink! Tomorrow you will understand. . . ."

He sprang like a devil out of his casket and smiled. His dazzling teeth looked like razor-sharp pen nibs. And he was coming closer and closer. . . .

I felt a dark veil descending slowly upon me.

six

Yum! Delicious . . .

Vampires don't exist. No one drinks a glass of blood for breakfast, and people sure don't suck ink with a straw. I hate these freaky nightmares. They make me jittery.

I had fallen asleep in my hiding spot. The bookstore was about to close. Two customers were still lingering in the store. A strong itch on my arm woke me up, and as I tried to get rid of it, I realized that it was coming from deep under my skin.

To make sure I had been dreaming, I browsed through a few books. Everything was in order. All the books were jam-packed with words. I returned to my hiding spot and felt overwhelmed by an indescribable mix of drowsiness and heaviness.

I heard my dad double-lock the store door. Alone at last!

The surrounding silence and darkness were exhilarating. Dad hadn't realized that I was still inside, and I was sure that once he did, he would search for me. But I had better things to do than go home to bed.

The books, all neatly lined up on the shelves, were calling me.

"Come, come, and open us!"

It was the very first time I had craved a book.

"Come, come and browse through us."

I just happened to have a straw in my pock-et. Lucky me!

The first mouthful was electrifying. However strange it may seem, I was eating sentences and crunching paragraphs. The books tasted like brownies!

Yum! Delicious!

But even more astounding, the sensations on my tongue varied from word to word, from paragraph to paragraph. I wasn't simply absorbing ink; I was absorbing pure and total adventure.

On a wild sea, two ships waged a ruthless battle. Crash! With swords between their teeth, the pirates smiled ferociously. I was not reading; I was experiencing all the action firsthand. I was the captain of the king's ship, and I was fighting for my life.

Suddenly I found myself facing a devil with an eye patch and a wooden leg. It was the notorious Captain Flint! We lunged at each other with our swords. I was exhausted. My arms felt like jelly. In a last-ditch effort, I rushed toward my enemy. He dodged my attack, and I went overboard. . . .

As I sucked the first words of the second paragraph, the lights were suddenly turned on. Dad was there. I swallowed wrong, and the words got stuck.

"Time for bed, little rascal," he said.

He didn't understand what I was doing with the book.

"You were supposed to read some books, not chew them!"

When he noticed the straw and the ink that was dripping down my chin, his anger subsided.

"Did a dog bite you?"

"Not exactly. . . ."

He must have feared I had rabies. I reassured him, claiming the ink was just chocolate. And he believed me!

Still, he wasn't totally wrong. I had indeed been bitten, but not by a dog. When I had passed out in the crypt, the vampire had used his niblike teeth to carve his name onto my arm. *Draculink* . . .

I was now one of his kind.

I had become an ink drinker.

And for the first time in my life, I relished being the son of a bookstore owner.

About the Author

ÉRIC SANVOISIN is one bizarre writer. Using a straw, he loves to suck the ink from all the fan letters he receives. That's what inspired him to write this story. He's sure that just as there are blood brothers and blood sisters, everyone who reads this book will become his ink brother or ink sister. If you write to him, he will send you a straw. That's a promise, or else he won't be writing again anytime soon.

About the Illustrator

If there's one thing MARTIN MATJE hates to do, it's write his biography. Biographies are just never much fun. So forget big dictionaries, this is one bio that's close to zero!